9/16

DATE DUE

MOUSE SCOUTS

Make a Difference

Sarah Dillard

A Yearling Book

Copyright © 2016 by Sarah Dillard
Melody for *The Acorn Scout Song* by Frank Fighera, lyrics by Sarah Dillard

All rights reserved. Published in the United States by Yearling,
an imprint of Random House Children's Books,
a division of Penguin Random House LLC, New York.

Yearling and the jumping horse design are registered trademarks
of Penguin Random House LLC.

Visit us on the Web! randomhousekids.com

Educators and librarians, for a variety of teaching tools, visit us at
RHTeachersLibrarians.com

Library of Congress Cataloging-in-Publication Data
Make a difference / Sarah Dillard. — First edition.
pages cm. — (Mouse Scouts ; 2)
Summary: "The Mouse Scouts are back for another badge. Violet, Tigerlily, and their friends are determined to earn their 'Make a Difference' badge."
—Provided by publisher
ISBN 978-0-385-75603-7 (trade) — ISBN 978-0-385-75605-1 (lib. bdg.)
ISBN 978-0-385-75604-4 (pbk.) — ISBN 978-0-385-75606-8 (ebook)
[1. Scouting (Youth activity)—Fiction. 2. Community life—Fiction.
3. Friendship—Fiction. 4. Mice—Fiction.] I. Title.
PZ7.D57733Mak 2016
[Fic]—dc23
2015009894

Printed in the United States of America
10 9 8 7 6 5 4 3 2 1
First Yearling Edition 2016

For my brother, Rob, a good scout

Contents

Chapter 1   *Make a Difference!*   1

Chapter 2   *Trouble with Trash*   13

Chapter 3   *What's the Difference?*   23

Chapter 4   *The Big Idea!*   39

Chapter 5   *Baskets!*   49

Chapter 6   *Squirrel Trouble*   63

Chapter 7   *A Cat in Need*   79

Chapter 8   *The Plan*   91

Chapter 9   *Making a BIG Difference*   103

Chapter 10   *Late!*   117

Epilogue   *The Badge Ceremony*   126

CHAPTER 1

∽

Make a Difference!

Violet was in heaven. In her opinion, craft time was one of the best parts of being a Mouse Scout. Today they were weaving baskets out of grass clippings. The fresh green scent tickled her nose as she wove the blades of grass over and under each other. Her basket would be beautiful! Violet could already imagine how happy her mother would be when she brought it home. Maybe they could fill it with juniper berries or flower petals and put it on the table in the front hall.

"Ugghh!" groaned Tigerlily. "Stupid grass clippings. What good are baskets anyway?" Violet glanced over at her friend. So far, Tigerlily's basket looked more like a clump of twisted grass.

"Oh, Tigerlily," said Violet. "Just be patient with it. And you're wrong. A basket can be *very* useful. Maybe you could put your tools in it or something."

"I'm going to use mine to gather crumbs," said Cricket with her mouth full. It wasn't even snack time yet, but Cricket had sneaked an acorn cracker when Miss Poppy wasn't looking.

"I'm going to use mine as a purse," said Hyacinth. "It will make a lovely accessory."

Petunia put her basket on her head and swanned around the table. "It's even better as a hat."

"PETUNIA!" Miss Poppy called out. Petunia stopped with a jerk, and the basket fell off her head, nearly taking her Acorn Scout cap with it.

"Baskets are not hats," said Miss Poppy. "I might expect that behavior from a Buttercup, but NOT from an Acorn Scout!"

Petunia blushed, and the other Scouts put their heads down and went back to work. All except for Junebug, who sat in the corner quietly reading the *Mouse Scout Monthly*. Junebug was allergic to

grass, so Miss Poppy had
said that she could skip the
day's craft.

"I wish *I* had allergies,"
Tigerlily muttered, giving
Junebug a sideways
glance. Tigerlily wrestled
some more with her clump of grass, but it
was no use. Her basket did not look anything like Violet's. No matter how hard
she tried, her crafts never came out right.

Tigerlily threw up her hands. "Why
can't we ever do *fun* stuff? When are
we going to do the 'Mousetrap Deploy-
ment' badge? Or the 'Puddle Navigation'
badge? When are we going to do something worthwhile?"

Violet frowned. She thought making

baskets was fun and very worthwhile. But Tigerlily was Tigerlily, and she wasn't going to be happy unless she was doing something death-defying.

Miss Poppy smiled. "As a matter of fact, you are about to embark on a very worthwhile project indeed. You are going to be working on your 'Make a Difference' badge."

"Make a difference?" Petunia asked. "Could you be a little more specific?"

"Ah!" Miss Poppy exclaimed. "That is the beauty of this badge. The difference you make will be up to you. It could be planting a small garden of perky flowers to spread a little sunshine in a dreary corner of town. It could be making a commitment to smile at someone new once a day. Small things can have big results. Even if all you do is brighten someone's day, you will have made a DIFFERENCE.

"BUT—there is more to this badge than sunshine and smiles. The 'Make a Difference' badge requires dedication to your community and a firm belief in your cause. This badge is about helping OTHERS. Be sure to keep a daily logbook of the differences you make, large or small. In addition, we will work on a project as a troop to make a significant difference in our community. That project is up to you Scouts to determine. Now get ready to go out there and . . . MAKE A DIFFERENCE! But first, snack time!"

All the Scouts except Tigerlily cheered, and helped themselves to snacks.

"Does anyone understand what we're supposed to be doing?" Tigerlily whispered to Violet.

"Making a difference?" Violet whispered back.

"But how are we going to do that?" asked Cricket.

"Who knows?" said Hyacinth.

"I certainly don't," said Petunia.

"Let's meet at the sandbox tomorrow," Violet suggested. "Everyone try to think of something we can do to make a differ-ence, and then we'll pick the best one."

When they were finished with their snacks, the Scouts got up and gath-ered their baskets—all except Junebug, who was engrossed in her *Mouse Scout Monthly*. She got up to leave and walked right into the craft table.

"Watch where you're going, Junebug!" cried Petunia. But Junebug was only pay-ing attention to the magazine. "Hmm," she muttered. "Fascinating."

MOUSE SCOUT HANDBOOK

YOU Can Make a Difference!

One of the greatest things that a Mouse Scout can do is to make a difference in her community. Whether leading a sing-along for the residents of an elder-mouse home, volunteering at a day-care center, or gathering nuts for the hungry, you are in a unique position as a Mouse Scout to make your community a better place.

By following
the Mouse Scout motto
of being
Cheerful,
Aware,
and **T**houghtful
(CAT, for short),
YOU can
make a difference!

CHAPTER 2

~_9

Trouble with Trash

As usual, Tigerlily was the first to leave the Mouse Scout meeting. She poked her head through the bushes outside the basement of the Left Meadow Elementary School and looked both ways. It paid to be careful about humans, cats, and other predators. "All clear!" she declared, and the rest of the Scouts tumbled out onto the school lawn. Hyacinth and Petunia

scampered off to the playground, and Cricket sniffed for crumbs. Junebug sat under a bush with her nose still buried in the *Mouse Scout Monthly*, while Violet and Tigerlily walked home together.

Violet had been hoping to pick some more grass for her baskets on the way home, but Tigerlily was in a grumpy mood.

"Leave it to Miss Poppy to take all the fun out of being a Mouse Scout," Tigerlily said. "I'm looking for adventure. I want action and excitement! We should be building canoes out of birch bark or learning survival skills. Instead, we have to do something *nice*. Why do we have to do that 'Make a Difference' badge, anyway?"

Sometimes Violet didn't understand Tigerlily. She *loved* the idea of the "Make a Difference" badge. She couldn't wait to get home and start her "Make a Difference" logbook. Imagine making a difference that could improve the community! Violet was determined to come up with the most amazing difference anyone had ever heard. All of the Scouts would be impressed. Even Miss Poppy would see what a great Scout she was!

Violet's heart swelled at the thought. *This might be my moment*, she was thinking when—*BLAM!* All at once, Violet was flat on the ground, her feet twisted in a plastic grocery bag.

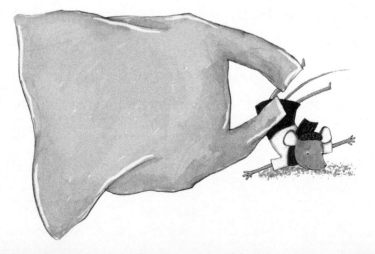

"Ouch! Where did *that* come from?" she squeaked. Tigerlily shook her head. Violet must have been day-dreaming again. When her friend got lost in thought, she could trip over her own tail, to say nothing about a plastic bag. It was a particularly nice bag, too, Tigerlily noticed. It looked sturdy and fairly clean, and there were no visible holes. "Hey, can I have that?" Tigerlily bent to pick it up before Violet could answer. "A bag like this could come in handy."

"It's just trash!" Violet said. "It's filthy!"

Tigerlily paid no attention to Violet. She was already imagining all sorts of possibilities for her new bag. It was so strong

17

that she thought she could twist it into a rope. And ropes were always useful. "See you tomorrow!" Tigerlily called as she scampered off, dragging the bag behind her.

"Make sure you wash your hands!" Violet called after her.

Violet stood up and brushed herself off, examining herself for injuries. Besides a slight dent in her acorn cap, everything seemed fine. "I *am* going to make a difference," she muttered. All she needed to do was figure out what that difference was going to be. She didn't have a single idea so far, but she was sure that *something* would come to her.

Before long, Violet's head was back in the clouds. So she didn't notice the cat watching her from across the street. She also didn't notice his tail swish as she ducked into the bush that covered her front door.

MOUSE SCOUT HANDBOOK

Trash Crafts

While mice are naturally tidy, we have to share the planet with creatures that are not as concerned about having a clean and healthy environment. How many times have you been enjoying a walk in the park, only to have it ruined when a blowing piece of trash knocks you over? Just because humans are careless and messy doesn't mean that mice have to suffer the consequences.

Humans are the greatest producers of trash in the animal kingdom. And you would be surprised by how much of what they discard can still be put to good use. Why let something be thrown away if it can be reused or recycled?

♪♫ With a little ingenuity, you can turn trash into treasures. Below are a few examples of inventive ways to use ordinary trash. But don't stop here. See what YOU can make from trash!

Bottle caps: bowls, planters

Fast-food containers: storage bins, bathtubs, wading pools

Water bottles: sprinklers

Straws: musical instruments, siphons, hoses

Mouse pads: carpets, exercise mats

Mousetraps: rowing machines

CHAPTER 3

What's the Difference?

When Violet woke up the next morning, an idea hit her: She knew exactly how the Mouse Scouts could make a difference! She was pretty sure everyone was going to love it. Well, everyone except for Tiger-lily. But she'd come around eventually. Violet put on her Mouse Scout uniform, grabbed a sunflower seed muffin, and ran out the door.

Tigerlily was walking up the sidewalk, dragging a plastic cup lid piled high with crumpled candy wrappers and bent coffee stirrers.

"What are you *doing*, Tigerlily?" Violet asked.

"I found these things for my collection," said Tigerlily. "You never know when you might find a use for something."

Violet sniffed. "Maybe you should be thinking about making a difference instead of collecting trash."

"I wish we were working on some other badge," said Tigerlily. "I have no idea how to make a difference! Have you thought of anything?"

Violet was dying to share her idea, but she knew better than to talk to Tigerlily about it without the others around. "I have a few ideas," she said. "Nothing special."

Tigerlily had already lost interest. She had just spotted another bottle cap for her collection.

When they got to the sandbox, the rest of the troop was already there. Hyacinth was holding a paper clip.

"Scouts, I have an idea!" Hyacinth

announced. "We can make a difference by giving other mice makeovers so they'll be as beautiful as me. Well, *almost* as beautiful, anyway. I'm going to start with Cricket."

Hyacinth took her paper clip and began to wrap Cricket's tail around it.

"Ouch!" said Cricket.

"Stop complaining," Hyacinth said.

"Not everyone can have a naturally curly tail like me. Sometimes it hurts to be beautiful."

But when Hyacinth pulled the paper clip away, Cricket's tail was as crooked as Petunia's.

"That made a difference, all right!" laughed Tigerlily. Cricket gave her a look and went to work shaking the kinks out of her tail.

"I don't think this is the kind of difference Miss Poppy meant," Petunia sniffed, trying to hide the fact that her feelings were a little hurt. She was very self-conscious about her own crooked tail, which was the result of a harrowing experience with a mousetrap. "We're supposed to do something that will make *others* feel happy. I know a few jokes. We could make a difference by making people laugh."

"I hope you don't mean your jokes about Miss Poppy," snorted Hyacinth. "You can't tell those."

"Oh," Petunia said. "I guess you're right. Back to the drawing board. Does anyone else have a great idea?"

Violet took a deep breath. It was now or never! "I think we should make baskets and fill them with flower petals and then give them to mice who are sad or needy, to brighten their day," she said breathlessly. She looked around. No one seemed as impressed as she had imagined they would be. Violet's nose began to twitch like it always did when she was nervous.

"Ugh. Not more baskets!" groaned Tigerlily.

"*Borrr*-ring," said Petunia.

BORRR-RING!

"They're right," said Hyacinth. "Besides, we've already made baskets. Next idea?"

Violet's tail drooped and she hung her head. She had been so sure that she had come up with a good idea! But now even she had to admit that making baskets wasn't much better than doing mouse makeovers or telling jokes. It wasn't going to change her community. It wasn't going to *make a difference*!

Junebug looked up from her copy of the *Mouse Scout Monthly.* "If we really wanted to make a difference, we'd be more like the Scouts featured in this magazine. We'd find a cure for cancer, or stop hunger, or clean up the environment."

"How can we do any of *those* things?"

Violet asked. "We're not grown-ups! We can't change the world. We might as well give up. We're only mice, after all."

"Oh no we're not!" said Tigerlily. She agreed with Junebug. If they had to go to the trouble of making a difference, it might as well be a really good one. "We're Mouse Scouts! It's just like in the Acorn Scout song. We may be small, but we're going to be tall, remember? Oh, you know how it goes. Anyway, if we put our minds to it and work together, we can come up with something that *will* make a difference."

Tigerlily smiled nervously as everyone turned to her. Just because she believed they could make a difference didn't mean she had any idea what that difference could be!

Suddenly, another plastic bag drifted across the sandbox and caught on Violet's acorn cap. "Yuck! Not another one!" she cried. "What is it with all of the trash around here, anyway? Someone should do something about this."

"That's it!" said Tigerlily. She knew *ex-actly* who should do something about it.

MOUSE SCOUT HANDBOOK

MICE WHO MADE A DIFFERENCE

DAISY   HYDRANGEA

Daisy and Hydrangea: The Mouse Scouts was established in 1953 by two mice named Daisy and Hydrangea. They formed an unlikely friendship after Hydrangea, a house mouse who had never been out of doors, was caught and released in a field far from home. When Daisy, an intrepid field mouse, found her, Hydrangea was cold and starving. Daisy nursed her back to health and taught her about wilderness survival, during which time Hydrangea developed a deep love for the natural world. These two visionary mice saw a need to instill a respect for the environment in young mice everywhere, in the hope that future generations of mice would be dedicated to preserving it.

Rosemary: The creator of the original recipe for Cheese Crispits was enjoying some cheese when she realized that she was late for a water safety lesson. She threw the cheese into her backpack, which was full of crumbs she had been collecting, and ran off to the birdbath in the park. There she spent several

ROSEMARY

hours practicing floating, diving, and treading water . . . while her backpack sat out in the hot sun. By the time her water safety lesson was done, the cheese in Rosemary's backpack had turned into a gooey, melted mess. Or had it? Rosemary was surprised to discover that when the melted cheese and crumbs cooled, they turned into a delicious crispy treat. Rosemary toyed with the recipe until she came up with Cheeso Delights, the popular Mouse Scout snack.

Olive, The Great Peacemaker: Throughout the late twentieth and early twenty-first centuries, the mice of Left Meadow were engaged in a conflict with squirrels and chipmunks over who could claim rights to the seeds spilled by careless birds at feeders. It took the courage of a strong leader and lifelong Mouse Scout, Olive, to broker a peace treaty. In 2003, after a series of meetings with the leaders of the chipmunk and squirrel nations—later referred to as the Seed Talks—an agreement was reached. It was decided that the first foot around the base of a bird feeder was for mice, the second foot in the perimeter for chipmunks, and the outer perimeter for squirrels.

OLIVE

CHAPTER 4

The Big Idea!

"We're going to take care of the trash!" Tigerlily said. "We'll make this park a place that everyone can enjoy without having to worry about being bombarded by litter."

"That's perfect!' said Cricket.

"I *guess* it will make a difference," Violet said. She still liked her basket idea better.

Tigerlily puffed out her chest and prepared to take charge. "Everyone spread out and look for trash. Drag everything you find to the trash can. Be sure to pay attention to anything that we might be able to reuse or recycle, and set it in a separate pile. We're going to clean up this place!"

The Scouts scurried around the park in search of trash. They didn't have to look very hard. Everywhere they went, they saw crumpled newspapers, plastic bags, greasy French fry containers, old socks, candy wrappers, potato chip bags, soda cans, and water bottles.

Petunia found a dented soda can and dragged it to the trash pile. Some of the soda dripped onto her uniform. "Ewww!" she squeaked.

Hyacinth found a paper cup and stuffed it with straws and wrappers that she picked up on her way to the trash pile.

Junebug kicked a plastic water bottle across the park. "I'm not touching this with my bare hands," she said. "It could be covered in contaminants."

Before long, the Scouts had made a large pile of trash next to the trash can.

"Look at all of this," said Junebug, pointing to a French fry container. "How do humans eat this stuff?"

Cricket hid the French fry she was nibbling behind her back. "It's not that bad, really."

"What a difference!" exclaimed Hyacinth a little while later. "I've never seen the park so clean!"

"Yeah," said Petunia. "It was filthy before."

"And very unhealthy," said Junebug. "Trash is a breeding ground for disease."

"This was one of the easiest badges ever!" said Tigerlily. "We cleaned up the park, which makes a difference for everyone. Plus, I got some great stuff for my collection!" Tigerlily was especially

43

excited about a roll of duct tape she had found under a bench. She had also found a chewed-up tennis ball, which was sure to be useful in one way or another.

Violet stood proudly by the trash pile and admired the nice clean park. They really *had* made a difference. She could already imagine mouse families spending happy afternoons building tunnels in the sandbox or napping under the shade of the daisies. She couldn't wait to go home and write about it in her "Make a Difference" logbook.

Just then, a breeze lifted a paper straw wrapper from the top of the pile and floated it down to the ground. As Violet looked at the trash again, she realized that they weren't quite done. "Oh no!"

she exclaimed. "All of that work was for nothing! We may have gathered the trash, but how are we going to get all of it *into* the can?"

MOUSE SCOUT HANDBOOK

Your "Make a Difference" Logbook

My
Make
a
Difference
Logbook

A fun way to keep track of the differences you make is to write them down! Keeping a daily logbook is easy once you get in the habit of it.

To begin your "Make a Difference" logbook, find an empty notebook, or make one yourself using the handy instructions on the next page.

1. Place a stack of lightweight paper between two pieces of heavy paper or poster board of the same size.

2. Punch five holes in your stack using a hole punch or awl.

3. Thread yarn through the holes.

4. Tie in knots.

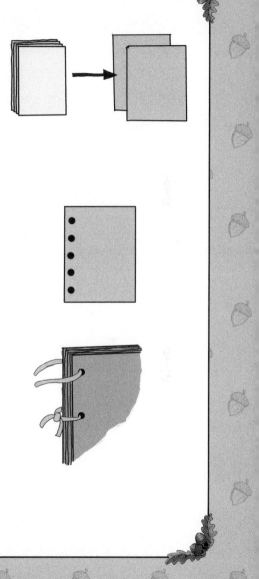

Once you have your logbook, you can start recording the differences you are making. Each night before you go to bed, write the date at the top of the page and think of everything you did that might have made a difference, then write it down. Next to these items, you can make a note of *how* it made a difference and *whom* it made a difference to.

After a week or so, look back at the entries in your logbook. You will be amazed at how many differences you can make!

CHAPTER 5

Baskets!

"Violet's right. We need to figure out a way to get the trash into the trash can," said Tigerlily.

"We could try throwing things up there," suggested Hyacinth. Even as she said it, Hyacinth did not sound convinced. "But none of us are probably strong enough. It would never work."

"If we could climb up the side of the

trash can, we could carry things up one by one," Petunia said. She took a running leap at the trash can, but it was too steep and too smooth to climb. She quickly slid to the ground.

"If I had some rope, we could make a ladder and get the trash up there," said Tigerlily.

She grabbed some plastic grocery bags and started twisting them.

When she had twisted three bags into strands, she began to braid the strands together to make a rope. It reminded Violet of the way she had made the handle for her grass clipping basket. . . .

"WAIT!" cried Violet. "I have an even better idea!"

The Scouts stopped and stared at her. Violet gulped and her nose twitched.

"Well?" said Hyacinth.

"We could make a basket," Violet squeaked.

Tigerlily put her hands to her head and groaned. "What is it with you and baskets?"

"Actually, it might work," Junebug said. "A smaller container would be more accessible. In fact, we could even make the *basket* out of trash. We'll twist the pieces together like Tigerlily's rope. Imagine, a basket, made of trash. *Holding* trash. We would be taking care of the trash problem and recycling at the same time. It would be something worthy of the *Mouse Scout Monthly*!"

"If that doesn't make a difference, I don't know what will," Cricket agreed.

Violet beamed.

Hyacinth and Petunia gathered all the plastic grocery bags, potato chip bags, and candy wrappers from the pile and set them aside, while Tigerlily and Cricket got to work braiding them into ropes.

As the pile of ropes grew, Violet took three long lengths of rope and laid them down in a star shape. She then took a fourth rope and began to weave it over and under the other three ropes.

Violet kept weaving until the base was as wide as four mice lying down end to end. Then the Scouts built up the sides. When the basket was mouse high, Violet climbed on Cricket's shoulders and kept weaving. Only when she couldn't reach any higher did they decide the basket was done.

The Scouts stood back and admired their basket. For something made out of trash, it was a thing of beauty. Violet had never felt so proud. Even Tigerlily was impressed. "Now *that's* a trash basket," she giggled.

Tigerlily climbed up the side of the basket and stood on the rim. The Scouts began to pass her the remaining trash piece by piece. Hyacinth and Petunia jumped up and down on the soda cans and water bottles to flatten them, and Cricket and Violet lifted them up to Tigerlily. Junebug raked the area around the trash basket with a plastic fork and then handed the fork to Tigerlily. When they were done, the basket was full and there wasn't a piece of trash to be seen anywhere.

But the Scouts weren't the only ones
admiring their work. From underneath
the bush he'd been napping in, a big red

cat looked on with interest. Now that the trash had been picked up, he had a better view of the Mouse Scouts. The cat licked his lips and purred.

MOUSE SCOUT HANDBOOK

How to Make a Basket

Imagine creating something that is both useful and beautiful from materials that you gather yourself! Making baskets from grass clippings or other found objects, such as flower stems or scraps of fabric, is easy once you know how. Follow the simple step-by-step guide below.

1. Gather your materials and, if necessary, braid or twist them to create lengths of rope.

2. Lay out three lengths of rope, crossing them in the middle. They will look like a six-armed star.

3. Starting in the center of your star, take another length of rope and weave it over and under the six arms, going around once as tightly as you can.

4. Next, insert a new length of rope into the center, so that your star has seven arms. An odd number of arms will help the basket hold its shape.

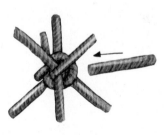

5. Continue to weave over and under the seven arms as tightly as possible to form the base of your basket. When you need to add a new length of rope, tuck the end of the piece you have been working with into the woven part, then insert the new rope in the same place.

6. When your base is the size that you want it to be, fold up the arms to create the sides.

7. Continue weaving until your basket has reached the height you want it to be.

8. Bend the arms over, one by one, and weave them into the top edge of the basket, creating a brim.

9. To create a handle, braid three lengths of rope together. Poke one end of the braid into the top of the basket and weave it in and out of your basket to the bottom so that it is secure. Repeat with the other end of the braid on the far side of the basket to form a handle.

Your finished basket will be something you will use forever. It would also make a lovely gift for a family member.

CHAPTER 6

❧

Squirrel Trouble

The next day, Violet skipped down the sidewalk. She was excited to get to her Mouse Scout meeting. Now that their "Make a Difference" project was done, the Scouts would receive their badges. She couldn't wait to sew the new badge onto her sash.

On her way to the school, Violet stopped at Tigerlily's house. She found her friend

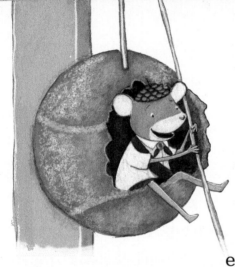

sitting in the chewed-up tennis ball she had discovered in the park. Tigerlily had rigged it with some twine, so that the ball was hanging from the porch rail. As Violet watched, Tigerlily pulled on the twine, and the tennis ball seat moved up!

"Hey, Violet! Look, I made an elevator!" Tigerlily called. "Want to try it?"

Violet did not. The twine didn't look very strong and the tennis ball looked tippy. She was surprised Tigerlily hadn't fallen out of it yet.

"I don't think so," Violet said. "I'm going to check on the trash basket before our meeting. We may need to pick up some more trash while we're there. Do you want to join me?"

Tigerlily thought about it. She was having fun, but the chance to find more treasures in the park was too good to pass up. She was hoping to find an old shoe that she could turn into a clubhouse. "Okay," she said, hopping out of her elevator.

As they neared the park, a Popsicle wrapper blew toward Violet. "I knew we'd find more trash," she said as she grabbed it. Then a crumpled potato chip bag nearly knocked her off her feet.

Next a bottle cap flew by and Tigerlily caught it like a Frisbee. "Hey!" she cried. "What is going on?"

"*Look!*" said Violet, pointing. A squirrel was sitting on top of their basket, throwing pieces of trash this way and that.

When the squirrel noticed Violet and Tigerlily, he gave a high-pitched laugh and started throwing popcorn at them.

"Let's get out of here," said Violet. "Squirrels scare me. They're not very nice and they're twice our size."

"No!" said Tigerlily. "I'm going to give that squirrel a piece of my mind. Just because he's bigger than us doesn't mean he can get away with ruining our 'Make a Difference.'"

Tigerlily took a deep breath, put her hands on her hips, and marched up to the trash basket. The squirrel looked down at her and laughed some more.

"We worked really hard to collect all that trash, squirrel, so you'd better get out of that trash can."

"Or else?" said the squirrel as he tried a sock on his head.

"Or else I'll . . ." But Tigerlily had no

idea what the "or else" was. "I'll . . . ," she started again. The squirrel leaned forward until his nose was inches away from Tigerlily.

"What can a little mouse do to *me*?" he giggled.

"I'll show you, you big . . . meanie!" Tigerlily couldn't believe she had said something so stupid. "I mean, you big . . ." But the squirrel had suddenly lost interest in Tigerlily's scolding. He was staring at something over her head.

Tigerlily turned around to see what could be so interesting. It was a cat. And not just any cat, but Big Red—the largest, meanest cat in the neighborhood. And Big Red was slowly creeping up behind Violet . . . and he looked ready to pounce.

"Violet!! CAT!" Tigerlily yelled.

"CAT?" Violet was puzzled. This did not seem to be the time for that particular Mouse Scout motto. "How can you expect me to be *Cheerful* at a time like this?"

Violet looked around and found her-

self face to face with Big Red. "Uh-oh."
She gulped. Big Red looked at Violet and
stretched out his paw.

"VIOLET!" Tigerlily drew her emergency whistle to her mouth. *PHWEEEET!!!*
"RUN!"

When Big Red heard the whistle, he looked toward Tigerlily and the squirrel. And when he saw the squirrel, he lost all interest in Violet.

"SQUIRREL!" growled Big Red.

As for the squirrel, he dropped the sock and ran for the nearest tree. Big Red bolted after him, knocking Tigerlily down as he ran by.

Tigerlily sat stunned on the ground.

"Are you okay?" Violet asked.

"I think so." Tigerlily rubbed her head and looked around. "But our trash basket isn't."

"Oh no!" Violet cried. Some of the trash that made up the basket had come loose, and most of the trash that had been in the basket was scattered all over the ground.

Tigerlily sighed and stood up. She dusted off her uniform and slowly started gathering trash. Violet made repairs to the basket and then helped Tigerlily.

"I think that does it," Tigerlily said, dropping one last candy wrapper into the trash basket.

"And just in time," said Violet. "If we leave right now, we might still make it to

the Mouse Scout meeting without being
late."

But as they turned to go, they heard a
loud, horrible yowl from high above their
heads.

MOUSE SCOUT HANDBOOK

~~~~~~~~~~~~~~~~~~~~~~~~~~~~~~~~~~~~~

Cat Safety

Cats are natural predators of mice. It is best to avoid them whenever possible. They cannot be reasoned with, and they are stubborn, willful, and unpredictable in temper. Cats who are used to being outdoors are especially threatening because they have honed lightning-fast reactions hunting birds, squirrels, and chipmunks. But mouse is their preferred delicacy.

Luckily, there are many ways that a mouse can outsmart a cat. If you come across a cat inside and are unable to duck into a mousehole, try running in tight, fast circles. The cat will at first be so mesmerized it will not attack. It will then become confused and slightly dizzy.

Take this opportunity to dash under the lowest piece of furniture you can find, and then carefully make your way to the nearest mousehole.

If for some reason you cannot run in a circle, try standing as still as a statue. Although cats have an astonishing ability to stare, transfixed, at something for hours, eventually even they will lose interest and walk away.

If you are outside, head for a stream, a puddle, or any body of water. Most cats do not like water. If there is no water nearby, duck into a chipmunk hole. This is not entirely desirable, as chipmunks rarely welcome unexpected visitors. However, once you have explained the purpose of your visit, the chipmunk will understand. Rodents usually bond together over their distrust of cats.

CHAPTER 7

A Cat in Need

"What *is* that?" Tigerlily asked. There was another yowl, followed by a sad little sob.

"It sounds like someone is hurt," Violet said.

Violet and Tigerlily looked up. Big Red was clinging to a branch high in the tree, holding on as hard as he could. He didn't look very mean anymore.

In fact, he looked like a scared and helpless kitten. Violet thought he even looked a tiny bit cute. From a distance, at least.

"Help me!" Big Red cried. "Somebody HELP ME!"

Tigerlily smirked. "He can stay up there, for all I care."

"HELLLP!" Big Red wailed. "Please?"

"Just climb down the way you went up," Violet suggested.

"I can't." Big Red whimpered and trembled. "I'm afraid of heights."

Tigerlily giggled. She couldn't help it. How could someone so big and mean be afraid of climbing down from a tree? She climbed up and down things all the time without even thinking about it.

Violet was more sympathetic. She knew what it was like to be afraid. "Maybe we should do something," she said.

"Why?" asked Tigerlily. "Cats are a nuisance. Besides, he was just about to pounce on you. He deserves what he gets."

Big Red whimpered again. Violet felt sorry for him in spite of herself.

"Well, we can't just leave him there," Violet said. "Didn't you read your *Mouse Scout Handbook*? To make a difference, we're supposed to be *helpful*, especially to those in need."

"We've already made a difference," said Tigerlily. "We cleaned up the park— twice! We don't need to do anything else. That badge is ours."

"But, Tigerlily, we have to help him."
Violet felt tears coming to her eyes. "He
needs us!"

Tigerlily hesitated. She didn't trust Big
Red, but she hated to see Violet upset.
Violet was Violet: If she saw a chance to
do good in the world, she was going to
take it. It was one of her most annoying
qualities.

Just then, Hyacinth and Petunia
walked by on their way to the school.

"Come on, you two," called Hyacinth. "It's almost time for the meeting."

Violet gasped. She had never been late to a meeting before. She had heard rumors about Miss Poppy sending mice back to Buttercups for being late—and she wasn't going to let that happen to her. But she also had to help Big Red. It was her Mouse Scout duty.

"We've got a situation, Scouts." Tigerlily pointed up at the tree. When they spotted the stranded cat, Hyacinth laughed and Petunia stuck her tongue out.

"I can't look down! It's making me dizzy!" Big Red wailed from above.

"Too bad, cat," said Hyacinth. "We've got more important things to do."

Cricket and Junebug scurried by, then

stopped when they saw the other Scouts.

"Almost . . . late . . . meeting," Junebug gasped. Running aggravated her asthma.

"Did we miss something?" Cricket asked. "Is the meeting in the park today?"

"No," squeaked Violet, and she pointed above her head and explained about Big Red.

"Even if we *wanted* to help him," said Cricket, "how could we ever get the cat down? We can't carry him, we're just little mice."

"I say we leave him there and go to our meeting," said Petunia, sticking out her tongue again. "It serves him right."

Tigerlily looked up at the tree. She had to admit, Big Red did look scared. But Cricket was right. How could they help? It was a terrible dilemma. *I should have just stayed in my elevator,* she thought.

Tigerlily looked at the trash basket. She looked up at the tree. Then she looked back at the basket.

"Hmmm . . . ," she said. "Could we . . . would it . . . ? Hold up, Mouse Scouts!" she shouted. "I have an idea!"

MOUSE SCOUT HANDBOOK

Teamwork

Some projects are too big for one mouse alone. But you are a Mouse Scout, and a Mouse Scout *always* has a team behind her. If you have an idea for a big project, propose it to your troop as something you can do as a team. When Mouse Scouts work together, they can accomplish almost anything!

A team works best when everyone has a specific task. Decide together what needs to be done and who will do what. If you finish your task before others, try to be helpful to another team member. Remember that you are not competing with your team members, you are all working together to accomplish something great. In a good team, every member is as important as everyone else.

Here is a fun game that will get you and your fellow Mouse Scouts working as a team.

Tied in Knots

1. Have everyone stand in a circle.

2. With your right hand, grab the tail of the Mouse Scout next to you. With your left hand, reach across the circle and grab someone else's left hand. It must not be the same mouse whose tail you are holding.

3. Without letting go, work together to untangle yourselves so that you are again standing in a circle.

CHAPTER 8

The Plan

"Listen up, Mouse Scouts," said Tiger-lily. "If we all pitch in, we'll have that cat down in no time at all. Wait here, I'll be right back. While I'm gone, take the trash out of the basket."

The Scouts watched her in disbelief.

"But we *just* put all the trash *in* the basket," said Cricket.

She was almost always agreeable, but this was getting to be too much.

"Is Tigerlily crazy?" Petunia asked.

"Probably," sighed Violet. The day had gone from bad to worse. It was very nearly time for their meeting, and it didn't look like they were going to make it. That meant she wasn't going to get her "Make a Difference" badge. But worst of all, Violet probably wasn't even going to be an Acorn

Is Tigerlily crazy?!

Probably.

Scout anymore. Since Miss Poppy didn't stand for lateness, she was most likely going to send them all back to Buttercups.

"I think we should forget about Tiger-lily," said Hyacinth. "Let's just go to the meeting." Hyacinth turned and started toward the Left Meadow Elementary School.

"I'm with Hyacinth," said Petunia as she scurried after her.

"It is physically impossible for us to do anything about that cat," said Junebug. "It goes against the laws of nature, not to mention gravity." She shrugged and fol-lowed Hyacinth and Petunia.

Cricket looked at Violet and shrugged. "The snack today is supposed to be ched-dar cheese. There's *nothing* better than

cheddar." She gave Violet one last plead-
ing look before running after the others.

Violet stood alone at the trash basket.
She couldn't believe Tigerlily cared that
much about the cat,
but Tigerlily was
Tigerlily, and when
she got a scheme in
her head, nothing else
mattered until it was
done. It was one of her
most annoying qualities.

Violet was torn. She
knew she should wait for
Tigerlily, but if she didn't follow the others . . . well, she couldn't bear the thought
of being a Buttercup again!

"I'm sorry, Tigerlily. Being an Acorn

Scout is just too important to me," Violet
whispered. She hoped she could catch up
to the other Scouts.

"HELLLLLP MEEEEE!" screeched the
cat.

Violet had nearly forgotten about Big
Red. He sounded more desperate than
ever. She remembered something she had
read in the *Mouse Scout Handbook:*

At times like this, a Mouse Scout must

use her inner resolve and put someone else's needs above her own.

"What was I thinking!" said Violet. "I *am* a true Mouse Scout. No matter what happens, we have to do the right thing."

"Come back!" she shouted to the other Scouts. "If anyone can figure out a way to rescue the cat, Tigerlily can. Miss Poppy will understand, she just has to!"

The other Scouts stopped and listened.

Violet had never sounded so sure of herself.

"Maybe she's right," sighed Hyacinth.

"What's the worst that could happen?" Petunia said with a shrug. "Buttercups wasn't *all* bad."

And with that, they all turned and hurried back to the trash basket.

A few minutes later, Tigerlily returned, dragging her emergency wagon behind

her. She pulled out a large ball of twine
and a long rope made of trash bags. She
tied them together, then tied one end
around her waist.

Tigerlily looked up at Big Red and gulped. She had never realized just how tall trees were.

Taking a deep breath, she said, "Okay, Scouts, I'm going up."

MOUSE SCOUT HANDBOOK

Your Emergency Tool Kit

Every Mouse Scout should have a collection of tools in case of emergency. You may keep your tools in a small box or any type of container that can hold them. It can be useful to keep the tools in a wagon, so that they are always readily available and transportable.

Once you have a container for your tools, you will need to fill it! Many ordinary objects can be useful in an emergency. Below are a few things to keep an eye out for and potential ways to use them. But don't stop there! Take a good look at any object you come across. With some creative thinking, there is no end to the purposes you might discover!

Duct tape: This is useful for repairs, or any situation where you need something sticky.

Toothpicks: Use them as levers, as walking sticks, and for deploying mousetraps.

Paper clips: With minimal bending, they can make a handy seat. Also good as snowshoes.

Elastics:

These are good for using as slingshots, bungee jumping, and holding things together.

Cheese: Every good tool kit should have emergency rations.

CHAPTER 9

Making a BIG Difference

"Be careful, Tigerlily!" Violet cried after her friend.

Tigerlily climbed straight up the trunk of the tree, dragging the rope behind her. But it was slow going. Twice she had to stop to untangle the rope from her tail. Plus, a mosquito was following her. "Get away!" she said, but the mosquito just kept buzzing.

When she reached the branch below Big Red, Tigerlily stopped to take a breath. She was exhausted! She looked up. It was still a long way to Big Red. She looked down. The ground was also very far away. "Just a little bit more," she told herself. "I'm almost there." The mosquito buzzed in her ear and tried to bite her acorn cap.

Slowly, Tigerlily inched up the trunk again. But just when she was nearly there, the mosquito landed on her nose. Tigerlily swatted it away—and lost her balance! She teetered back and forth and just managed to grab on to a leaf. But she could not pull herself up to Big Red's branch.

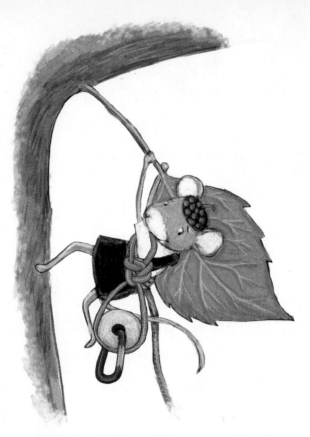

"Help!" Tigerlily squeaked.

Big Red looked down. This was an unusual situation for him. He was more used
to chasing mice than helping them. He
wasn't sure what to do.

Tigerlily was exasperated. "Look, cat. Do you want to get out of this tree or not?"

Big Red couldn't believe what he was hearing. "Are you here to *rescue* me?" For a minute, he felt bad that he had been thinking of chasing mice. And then he laughed. "That's impossible."

"You'll never know if you don't help me," said Tigerlily.

Big Red looked at Tigerlily. Then he looked past her to the ground far, *far* below—and quickly pinched his eyes shut. His stomach flipped and his legs felt like jelly. The thought of trying to get down the tree by himself made him dizzy. He opened one eye and looked at Tigerlily again. She was just a tiny little mouse. But Big Red was so desperate he was willing to try anything. He carefully stretched a paw toward the leaf where Tigerlily was hanging. Tigerlily quickly jumped onto his paw and he lifted it back to his own branch.

"Thanks," Tigerlily said.

"Don't mention it," Big Red replied, feeling oddly humbled. No one had ever thanked him for anything before. "But I don't really see how you can help me. *You* are a tiny little mouse. *I* am a pretty big cat. You'll never be able to do this by yourself."

"Just wait, you'll see," said Tigerlily. And with that, she looped the twine over the branch and began to rappel down the tree, quickly reaching the ground and the rest of the Scouts.

"Are you *sure* this is a good idea?" asked Petunia.

"He's probably hungry," said Cricket. "We must look delicious to him."

"I'm pretty sure we can trust him," said Tigerlily. "But be prepared to run just the same."

paper clip

Tinkertoy

Tinkertoy

carabiner

Tigerlily took the end of the rope and tied it securely to the basket. Then she turned over her emergency wagon and looped the rope around two of the wheels. Using a wooden clothespin, rubber bands, and other items, she devised a pulley.

"Everyone grab on to the rope!" Tigerlily shouted. "And when I say 'pull,' *pull!*" The Scouts took position.

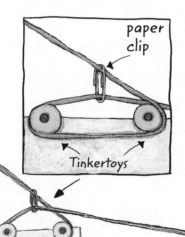

paper clip

Tinkertoys

"Okay, cat!" Tigerlily shouted up to Big Red. "Wait for the basket."

Big Red looked down. It was a *long* way to the ground.

Following Tigerlily's lead, the Scouts pulled on the rope. Slowly, the basket began to rise, and before long it was just below Big Red's branch.

Big Red looked at the basket. Was it made out of . . . *trash?* Gingerly, he reached a paw out to the basket. It crinkled when he touched it. *That will never hold me,* he thought. But spending the rest of his life in the tree seemed even worse than trying to get himself into the basket. Slowly . . . carefully . . . he stepped off the branch and into the basket.

"Here goes nothing!"

The Scouts cheered when the basket reached the ground and Big Red stepped

out, unharmed. "That was just like something you would read about in the *Mouse Scout Monthly*!" Junebug exclaimed.

"We should tell Miss Poppy. Maybe she'll write to the magazine!" Cricket joined in.

"Miss Poppy!" Violet gasped. "OH NO! We're late for Mouse Scouts. WE'RE GOING TO BE SENT BACK TO BUTTERCUPS!"

"Maybe *I* can help," said Big Red.

MOUSE SCOUT HANDBOOK

Helping Others

One of the greatest ways that a Mouse Scout can make a difference is to help those in need. Whether you are assisting a neighbor stack a pile of nuts, bringing some cheese to a mouse who is sick, or simply clearing a leaf away from someone's door, your consideration can make another mouse's life easier and brighter.

Sometimes, a Scout may come across someone in real trouble, and providing assistance may not be easy and can require great courage. Perhaps you see a Buttercup Scout

who is stuck in the
middle of a puddle
and cannot swim.
Or maybe another
animal is in distress,

such as a bat trapped in a wall with no idea
how to get out, or a snapping turtle who has
managed to flip himself onto his back and is
unable to turn himself right side up. At times
like this, a Mouse Scout must use her inner
resolve and *put someone else's needs above
her own.* As the Acorn Scout song says,
"We're quick with a plan, and we help when
we can." And always remember, someday you
might need some help yourself.

Here is a fun game to encourage you to
be aware of the needs of others. At a Mouse
Scout meeting, write down every Scout's

name on a piece of paper and put it in a hat. Every Scout will draw a name, and that person will be your secret buddy. From that meeting until the next, pay attention to your buddy and think of ways that you can help her. See if you can do it without your buddy figuring it out! At the next Mouse Scout meeting, all secret buddies will be revealed.

CHAPTER 10

〜

Late!

Miss Poppy looked at the clock. It was ten minutes after three o'clock and not one of her Scouts had shown up for the meeting. She peered through a crack in the foundation: not a mouse in sight!

"Maybe it was too soon to have them work on their

'Make a Difference' badge," Miss Poppy muttered. "The Scouts aren't ready for that kind of independence. They clearly need more structure. If they don't arrive soon, I have half a mind to send them all back to Buttercups!"

But Miss Poppy's frustration turned to worry when she saw Big Red round the corner to the school. A cat on the move was never a good sign. In fact, what if the cat had something to do with her Scouts being late? Miss Poppy reached for her emergency whistle and was just about to blow into it when she noticed something unusual about the cat.

There, on Big Red's back, waving, were all six of her Mouse Scouts.

"Well, I never!" she gasped.

Suddenly, out of nowhere, came the blur of a furry tail.

"SQUIRREL!" Big Red hissed. And just like that, he bounded after the squirrel—sending the Mouse Scouts flying from his back. They landed in a heap right in front of Miss Poppy.

Miss Poppy stood over the pile of Mouse
Scouts.

"YOU'RE LATE!" she said.

The Scouts hurried to their feet and stood at attention. Violet started to tremble. Was this the end? Was her worst nightmare about to come true? "Are you sending us back to Buttercups?" she squeaked.

"Am I—I . . . what?" stammered Miss Poppy. "No, of course not. I mean, not *this* time. Something tells me you had a good reason for your tardiness. Now, come inside and tell me what you have been doing to earn your 'Make a Difference' badge."

MOUSE SCOUT HANDBOOK

Punctuality

A Mouse Scout prides herself on punctuality. It is as important as trustworthiness and honesty. That's because a Mouse Scout who is always on time can usually be depended on.

A Mouse Scout who is punctual is also almost always organized and tidy. She keeps a calendar of important dates, such as birthdays and Mouse Scout holidays, so she is never caught unprepared. She is aware of the time and keeps track of how long it takes to get somewhere. And she always leaves herself a little extra time in case of unexpected delays— or a sudden discovery of cheese.

A Mouse Scout who is usually tardy is easy

to spot. She is often out of breath, her uniform is askew, and she tends to be forgetful. If there are mice in your troop who have trouble with punctuality, try to be helpful by reminding them of important dates and times. While punctuality does not come naturally to all mice, with some awareness, it can be learned!

EPILOGUE

◦～◦

The Badge Ceremony

From the *Mouse Scout Monthly*

MOUSE SCOUTS MAKE A DIFFERENCE IN THEIR COMMUNITY

LEFT MEADOW: Six Acorn Scouts in Left Meadow recently completed work on their "Make a Difference" badge by cleaning up a local park. But this was no ordinary cleanup. In addition to collecting trash, the Scouts used some of the trash to weave a basket to hold yet more trash, giving new meaning to the phrase *trash basket*.

"The 'Make a Difference' badge is a difficult one to earn," explained troop leader Miss Poppy. "The Scouts must determine what kind of difference they will make and how they will carry it out. Many troops simply aren't ready for that level of independence and responsibility, but I never doubted that MY scouts could handle it."

In fact, Miss Poppy's Scouts went above and beyond the requirements of the badge when the troop members discovered a local cat, Big Red, stuck in a tree. Working together, the Scouts came up with a plan to lower the cat to safety. "My Scouts are clever and fearless," Miss Poppy said. "They risked life and limb to help a creature in need. They are true Mouse Scouts!"

When asked for a comment, one of the troop members, Tigerlily, stepped forward. Showing true Mouse Scout modesty, she said, "We were happy to help. Besides, it was worth it to ride on a cat!"

MOUSE SCOUT HANDBOOK

THE "MAKE A DIFFERENCE" BADGE

To earn this badge, you must complete the following activities:

1. Keep a daily logbook of the little differences that you make.

2. With members from your troop, devise a plan for making a significant difference in your community.

3. Be an active member of your troop's "Make a Difference" team.

4. Write a short essay describing the significant difference your Mouse Scout troop made, including how you came up with your plan, how you carried out your plan, and what effect your difference made in your community.

MOUSE SCOUT BADGES

Sow It and Grow It

Mouse Scout Heritage

Fun and Foraging

Make a Difference

Baking with Seeds

Take Flight

Dramatics

Signs of Fall

First Aid

Winter Safety

Predator Awareness

Camp Out

Flower Fashions

Weaving with Grass

The Night Sky

Friendship

THE ACORN SCOUT SONG

Melody by Frank Fighera

We are A – corns, ti – ny and small, but we'll grow up to be migh – ty and tall. We're quick with a plan, and we help when we can. We love our friends and are kind to all.